In Dockleaf Cottage, crouched among the tangled weeds of Dockleaf Lane with its hundred potholes, live Miss Petunia Pennefeather & Cat. She's supposed to be a witch but Furball sometime wonders ...

What happens when she makes Spell 900 instead of Spell 600? Well, what happens is Victoria (the Hon. Victoria Elena Ross-O'Brien), Tansy and Joey ... Petunia reads the Riot Act but can keep Spell 101 (How to Make Unwanted Persons Disappear) going, and the children win Round One.

Petunia intends to win the war but she has other problems, notably Ivy ffrench-Fawcett who can do everything she can't, including ... (but that's a secret known only to Furball).

Dinner at eight with Spook cocktail is a wild success. But PP misses out on TV's *Places and Faces* and vows revenge. The *Garden Village of the Year* award is looming up and everyone is afraid of what is lurking behind the newly erected barricades at Dockleaf.

Meanwhile, who will get the coveted role of Superman's Granny in the Otis B. Henneberry big-budget movie? And will poor Furball ever escape ...?

Terry Hassett Henry

The Witch
who couldn't

Illustrated by Terry Myler

THE CHILDREN'S PRESS

To Victoria and Chloe

First published 1988 by
The Children's Press
45 Palmerston Road, Dublin 6
This edition 1991
Reprinted 1994

ISBN 0 947962 65 4 paper

Typesetting by Computertype Limited
Printed by Colour Books Limited

Contents

1

Dockleaf Cottage

Dockleaf Cottage crouched among the tangled weeds and crab-appled trees right at the end of Dockleaf Lane. To actually find the old house you had to follow a narrow lane which wound its way around clumps of large green quilted hosta leaves.

It was a most unusual lane, as someone had carefully dug a hundred potholes in it. Each one had a little stone set in on the top, with the number painted on. There were some goldfish swimming in No. 11, some faded comics and postcards in No. 27, a pair of muddy green wellies in No. 65, and an entire beetle family in No. 99, by the gate.

Anyone passing Dockleaf Cottage would probably have wondered just who lived there, in such an odd manner. Outside the gate of this old and rather badly built stone cottage, with its drooping windows and lop-sided gables, was a rusty nameplate which read,

Miss Petunia Pennefeather & Cat

Petunia ('Penny' to her friends, if indeed she had any) and her cat, Furball, had lived together for such a long time that neither could remember a time when they hadn't.

Inside the cottage, which always managed to look as if it had been built on a lazy afternoon and nobody had been too bothered how it turned out, Furball sat on the dusty window-sill one beautiful June evening. Only his furry tail could be seen from behind the large book he was reading with great interest. The name of the book was *Great Cat Escapes of the 1880s*, and it was his most prized treasure. It had been left to him by his long-lost father Saltypaws, who had been a ship's cat aboard a deadly pirate ship and had sailed the world.

'Now, there was a cat!' thought Furball wistfully.

The small finely boned cat stretched out his thin body of salt and pepper fur. His tousled face always appeared to wear a rather surprised look, as if he had just received a nasty shock. And as he lived with Miss Petunia Penne-feather, was it any wonder?

As he finished his book, his eyes grew soft and dreamy and he sighed deeply as he put it away and glanced around the untidy room.

'One day I'll escape,' he thought, 'and lead an exciting life . . . just like dear old Da . . .'

The sound of a voice shrilling his name startled him so much that he almost fell off the ledge. His eyes, following the sound, came to rest on his mistress.

Now, not many people knew this, but Miss Petunia Pennefeather was a witch. She was a small, thin, bony woman, with a pale face and small, black, bird-like eyes which seemed to be able to see everywhere at once. But perhaps the strangest thing about the witch was her hair. It wasn't too long or straight or black like most witches' hair. Oh, no! Petunia's hair was grey and she wore it in five ringlets; two long curly ones on either side of her face, and a large fat one down her back.

'Who ever heard of a witch with ringlets?' thought Furball in disgust.

'Furball! Furball!' shrilled the witch again. 'Where are you, you tatty bag of fur?'

She began searching about the kitchen, under the old wooden dresser loaded with all sorts of cracked plates, and among the faded cushions on the lumpy armchairs each side of the big old iron stove. Not finding him she went into the seldom used dining-room and began searching in there. She looked under the long sideboard which was cluttered with dust-covered glassware and odd bits of silver and cutlery that she had somehow 'found' in her pockets after one of her trips to town.

Still looking and shouting, she crossed the hall and went into her bedroom. What a place! Furball shuddered at the thought of it. He had been there a couple of times and it was not a pretty sight. A great big black satin quilt clung to the sagging bed. Five fat lumpy pillows edged with black lace sat on the bed, which was higher at the top than the bottom. The entire room was papered in spiderweb wallpaper, and the only bright spot was a large poster of Superman over her brass bedhead — Petunia was absolutely crackers about Superman.

Rattling the curtain in the little bathroom off her bedroom she disturbed a family of frogs who lived in the shower. She never used it; she only ever gave herself a 'cat lick', with the odd squirt of furniture polish behind the ears. 'Washing robs the skin of its natural oils,' she used to say. 'Leads to wrinkles at an early age!'

Finally she rounded into the parlour, a cold musty old room which always smelt a bit like a museum,

mused Furball, thinking of the spindly antique furniture and silk cushions, looked down on by some very
mysterious-looking ladies and gentlemen who appeared,
if their expressions were anything to go by, to have
just eaten something awful.

On and on chundered the witch as she searched
among the creeping ivy plant, which had not only crept
up its pole to the ceiling but had wandered everywhere
and now clung to wall-lamps and curtain rails until the
room resembled a green Japanese hanging garden.

Furball had often wondered about the pack of
playing-cards on the small green felt table on which
someone had been playing 'poker', but as they too were
covered in the usual grey clouds of dust he decided
it couldn't have been Petunia. Probably one of the
ancestors; maybe this was the very hand which had cost
the Pennefeathers their lands and estates, reducing
Petunia from the grandeur of Creaky Hall to the grim
penury of Dockleaf Cottage. Because Petunia hadn't
always lived here; once she had been very grand indeed.

Returning to the kitchen, the witch muttered loudly,
'Drat that cat! He's always trying to escape!'

Furball sat quite silent and still, shrinking in behind
a seldom opened volume, *101 Wonderful Work-outs for
Witches*. He knew the witch had terribly poor eyesight,
and although she wouldn't admit to needing glasses,
she really couldn't see very well, especially in the
gloomy kitchen. Scurrying about in her long grey dress
with wrapover striped apron she went on, 'I just can't
spent any more time looking for that wretched Furbag.
I'm so much behind in my spell-making.'

The cat watched as she scooted around the old
wooden furniture in search of her spell-recipe book,
disturbing everything on the big table which was littered

with large pewter spoons and ladles and mixing bowls, with some rather odd-shaped jars at one end.

Pawing his whiskers, he thought to himself, 'Why does she go on with her spell-making like an ordinary witch?' He knew that she hadn't done anything remotely magical or mysterious in years. In fact she hadn't ridden a broomstick in . . .

'Snooks!' snapped the witch, as she finally found her recipe book on a shelf under a jar of mind-your-own-business jelly. Then opening up a page hurriedly and looking at it very quickly she busied herself at the spell business.

Furball didn't quite catch everything she was muttering but he did hear some words here and there, 'A pair of frog's nail clippings . . . a couple of mice whiskers . . . two spiders' blisters . . . a large and smelly sock . . .'

'Ugh!' he thought. 'It sounds a truly awful recipe!'

As he watched Penny he wondered what would happen this time; he often wondered at the things she did!

The witch, having mixed up her nauseous ingredients, flung them into a cooking tin and scurried over to the big old stove. Putting it in she clanked the heavy door shut.

'Now!' she cackled. 'Now, one hour to wait for a truly powerful spell ... and of course Spell 600 is one of my favourites.'

'Liar!' thought Furball. 'It was a mess last time round.'

Squinting over towards the window the witch snapped to the cat she'd forgotten she couldn't find, 'Furball! I'm going to have a little snooze in my ball-of-string chair.'

This was her favourite chair for sitting in and thinking, and more often than not snoozing. It was made entirely from holes tied together with string, and it hung from a beam in the ceiling.

As she eased herself into it, she rapped, 'Wake me up in exactly ONE HOUR, Tattyfur.' and then fell promptly asleep, muttering to herself, 'Wind–tunnels and air-pockets ... wind-tunnels and ... zzzz ...'

The cat didn't move until he was very sure she was asleep. Then he slid down and went over to the table to lick the mixing-plate clean — catfood was a luxury in Dockleaf Cottage and poor Furball had to live off the country, not to mention the scrapings of her ladyship's spells.

'Ugh!' he moaned on tasting the remains of the recipe. 'Inedible! That's what that is!'

Pushing away the plate he couldn't help thinking

aloud, 'She's the meanest, silliest witch in the world ... Always dreaming and planning schemes that will impress everyone with her witch-like powers, when really all she does is end up making a fool of herself! Why,' he went on, 'if she ever suspects anyone is having fun she makes them disappear ... or tries to. And, of course, what upsets her most are children. Boys and girls, even babies, have been known to send her berserk.'

This was indeed true. The Pennefeather family motto was *Omnes Libri Germines Taetres*, which a reliable source had translated for Furball as, 'All children are disgusting germs!'

All of a sudden there seemed to be knocking and shouting coming from inside the oven. The noise grew so loud that it finally woke the witch who groaned sleepily, 'What time is it?'

As she climbed out of her chair she yawned, 'Where are my oven gloves? Is that you whinging again, Furbrain? Is that what the noise is?'

Furball shook his head as if saying, 'It's not me, Penny — the noise seems to be coming from INSIDE the oven.'

'Ah, snooks!' scoffed the witch as she opened the oven door.

Then she jumped back so quickly that she fell right on top of Furball who was following her, almost squashing him flat. The witch and the cat lay on the floor where they had fallen, and then their eyes grew wide ... and then wider ... for climbing out of the oven were CHILDREN!

2
A Mean Old Witch

The first child was a pretty girl with bluebell eyes and curly corn-coloured hair which tumbled all over the shoulders of her old-fashioned, deep blue velvet dress. Underneath a collection of grubby white petticoats peeped around her knees, above blue silk stockings which tapered into pale blue satin pumps. She looked around the kitchen in a haughty manner and then spoke in a cool crisp voice, holding out a dainty gloved hand, 'Good afternoon, my name is Miss Victoria . . .'

The witch could only stare at her, hand to mouth, before the second child interrupted, 'Oh! And my name's Tansy.'

The voice belonged to a smaller slender girl in a dirt-smeared simple brown smock dress. Dark brown eyes sparkled above her freckled nose and her rather lop-sided pigtails wriggled playfully; she smiled brightly as if among friends.

A funny noise was still coming from the oven. Then, as it began to get louder, it sounded like someone whistling. Whistling that was very thin and very out of tune. A torn trouser leg appeared from inside the oven and everyone in the kitchen stood silent and waited.

Out came a boy of about ten or eleven who looked as if he had grown too big for his clothes. He had tufts of blue-black hair and was probably bursting with mischief, if the snapping eyes and snagged clothes were anything to go by. He touched his forelock to nobody

Good afternoon, my name is Victoria...

in particular and joined the two girls. They stared at each other, at their surroundings, at the cat and, in turn, surreptitiously at the witch, who was still looking stunned.

Suddenly, scrambling to her feet, she roared in a terrible rage, 'What ... what do you think you're doing here in my stove? In my kitchen? Dressed in such old-fashioned clothes. You ...' she faltered as Tansy rushed towards her waving her arms.

'We're free! We're free at last! After being stuck in time for over a hundred years.'

'Stuck? In time? A hundred years ...?' croaked the witch hoarsely.

'Yes ... yes,' went on Tansy excitedly. 'You see we were all together ...'

'. . . in the grounds of my father's estate,' interrupted Victoria. 'You see, Daddy's Sir Basil Ross-O'Brien. I was having afternoon tea on the lawn and Tansy, one of the kitchen-maids, had just brought me out an éclair that the butler had forgotten. And my pony was just being brought around by this . . . stable-boy . . . called Andy or Paddy or Joe . . .'

'Joey,' supplied the urchin.

'Spare me the gruesome details,' hissed the witch, hardly able to speak with rage.

'Somebody,' continued Victoria, 'is responsible for this mess, and when my Daddy, Sir Basil Ross-O'Brien, finds out *who*, heads will roll!'

Without warning, Tansy rushed over to Petunia, and throwing her arms around the witch's bony body she said delightedly, 'Oh, but you must be the kind-hearted person who set us free! Oh, let me hug you, and from now on we shall be *your* children.'

Furball hurriedly covered his head, expecting the witch to explode from temper. He didn't have long to wait . . .

'Stop this hugging and kissing AT ONCE!' bellowed the witch, rubbing her sleeve hard where the little girl had touched her. 'Stop this at once, you pesky pests! You grotty little germs! Stop or I'll . . .'

'Don't worry, mother,' whispered Tansy. 'It's been a shock. But you'll soon get used to us. At last we have a kind mother again.'

The witch shivered and shook with temper. Her pale face grew red with rage and her ringlets danced as she howled, 'I'm not your mother. I'm Petunia Pennefeather, a mean old witch, and I haven't got a kind bone in my body. And what's more . . . I'm proud of it!'

As the children looked at her in amazement, she continued, 'Now get back in that oven at once ... or I'll ...'

Tansy burst into tears and Joey took a step backwards. But Victoria drew herself up tall and said haughtily, 'We won't. *You* sent for us. We're here because of you!'

Petunia slowly sank into her ball-of-string chair as Victoria went on, 'You made Spell 900.'

'Spell 900? Spell 900!' shouted the witch. 'I didn't make Spell 900. I made Spell 600!'

'Then why are we here?' Victoria asked relentlessly. 'It's quite clear ... you made a mistake.'

Furball almost choked with giggles as he jammed his paw between his teeth.

'Snooks and solo flights,' hissed the witch. 'It's all that cat's fault. If he hadn't been missing all morning I wouldn't have been in such a tizzy with my spell-making.' Reaching out with her long pointed shoes she tried to poke the poor old cat in the ribs but missed by a whisker. 'Not another fish-head for you until the year 2000, Hairbag.'

'Ahem ... ahem ... Miss Witch,' trembled Tansy, 'What's Spell 600?'

A great big smile broke over the witch's face at this question. Smiling (well, as well as she could without teeth) she answered a trifle dreamily, 'Spell 600? Spell 600 is for Misery and Unhappiness. One teaspoon of that recipe and you're *miserable* for life! My mother,' she continued, 'made sure I had plenty of it when I was young.'

No one said anything for a long time, and the only sound in the kitchen was the grinding of the witch's gums. She kept her teeth in an empty sugar-bowl as she found them uncomfortable, which didn't half startle visitors to whom she inadvertently served it up with cream and tea.

'What now?' thought Furball, as the witch seemed sunk in a trance.

Suddenly she leaped to her feet, pointed a piercing finger at the children and said, 'Begone! I'm going to leave the room for a few minutes. If you're still here when I get back ... BEWARE!' And muttering to herself, 'Children! Dirty loathsome things! Noise! Fingerprints everywhere! Football! Broken glass! Clothes thrown on the floor! Expense! Ingratitude! Whistling!' she swept out of the kitchen, sending the aspidistra in the hall flying in all directions.

3

A Battle of Wits

'We're obviously going to have more Spells,' thought Furball when the witch had disappeared. 'Maybe I can fit in a catnap first. It's been a most disturbing morning.'

Tansy and Joey clustered around Victoria.

'Oh, Miss, . . . what are we going to do ?'

'Oh, Miss . . . she'll put us back in the oven . . .'

'. . . and we'll be floating around for another hundred years . . .'

'. . . and we'll never get back to earth again. . .'

'Rubbish!' said Victoria. 'Listen to me. There's not a thing she can do about us. We're here . . . and here we're going to stay.'

'What about her magic?' sobbed Tansy.

'She *did* get us back to earth,' whispered Joey.

'Oh, that,' scoffed Victoria. 'Well, if you make 1000 spells a year you're bound to get one right — by mistake.'

'Got it in one,' thought Furball sleepily. 'Smart girl, that!'

'Oh, Miss,' began Tansy, starting to sob again.

'Turn off the waterworks!' commanded Victoria. 'Leave this to me . . . shss . . . I hear her coming back .'

It was indeed Petunia who slithered back sideways like a crab, eyes half-closed. Then she saw the children still standing there and leaped three feet in the air.

'I won't have it!' she roared, waking up the poor old cat. Catching sight of Joey's grinning face, she

19

ground her teeth and threw a plate at him. Luckily he ducked. 'But then he would,' thought Victoria. 'He's used to that sort of thing.'

'I won't have it,' roared the witch. 'Where's my recipe book ... just you wait ... Spell 101 ... How to Make Unwanted Persons Disappear ... that'll fix you all ...'

'Oh, dear,' thought Furball in dismay as she leafed through the book. 'What's she going to do when she finds out that. . .?'

Petunia was just about to find out. The book was now open at Spell 101:

HOW TO MAK
UNWANTED PE
DISAP

The rest of the page had been torn away.

'That was the time she tried to make Ivy ffrench-Fawcett disappear,' thought Furball, 'and it didn't work so she bit the page to shreds. What's going to happen now?'

He put his paws over his ears just in time.

With a piercing shriek that made Joey dive under the table, Petunia sank down into her ball-of-string chair, temporarily winded. Victoria seized her chance.

'I think,' she said in the cool crisp tones she had heard her mother use when addressing Members of the Lower Orders, 'I think we should come to some kind of arrangement.'

'With you? You grotty germs? Do you think I'll ...'

'Just think of how helpful we could be to you,' Victoria's voice was silkily persuasive. 'We could clean ... cook ... make the beds ... scrub the floors ... wash the dishes ... dust ...' Victoria ran a practised finger along the dresser, leaving a thin black track through

the grey, '... run messages for you ... call you in the morning ... bring you afternoon tea ...'

Not that Victoria meant to do any of the work herself, of course. She had been trained in How to Handle Servants and meant to put the lessons into practice!

'And, of course,' continued Victoria, seeing signs of wavering, 'we'd sleep in the attic or in the tool-shed or wherever you choose, so we wouldn't be in your way ... why you'd hardly ever see us. We'd be your invisible army of servants. You'd live just as in the good old days ... servants at your beck and call...'

She had touched the magic chord! Hidden so deeply Petunia Pennefeather had almost forgotten it was there. She seemed to blossom — for a moment. 'Well, naturally, I was always used to better things...' She had a sudden vision of a neat little maid serving her

J61070.

cucumber sandwiches and anchovies on toast triangles and *Lapsang Souchong* tea in wafer-thin china.

Naturally, being Petunia, she found this sweetness and light difficult to maintain for more than a minute. She was soon her old self, screeching loudly, 'You lot! Sit down and stop cluttering up the place. Furball, fetch me a fine fresh nettle from the garden.'

The little cat scampered off at top speed and soon reappeared carrying a large very green nettle from the garden. This he laid on the table for the witch's inspection. Satisfied that it was really fresh, Petunia rounded on Victoria saying, 'Hey you, blue stockings! Make me a nice drop of herbal tea. And mind it's piping hot!'

Victoria turned to Joey. 'Boy,' she began, 'get. . .'

'No!' scowled the witch. 'Not that half-wit. YOU! You're to make the tea.'

There was a moment's horrified silence. Tansy and Joey were afraid to breathe — would Miss Victoria . . . could Miss Victoria . . . act the servant girl? Victoria finally swallowed hard, muttered something under her breath and went to get the hot water.

Petunia, still scowling, went on grumbling. 'What a day this has turned out to be, almost as bad as black-and-grey Monday in 1903. Those interfering Wright Brothers had no business at all inventing two-winged planes. They're the cause of it all . . . cluttering up the air-lanes . . . yap, yap . . . .'

Furball, fearing he would have to hear the tale of 1903 for the 997th time, hurriedly took her the evening paper. Yesterday's evening paper; a well-known witch custom that Penny followed with enthusiasm. She began turning the pages furiously, muttering 'Bah!' and 'Snooks!' every now and then. As she was behind the paper, she didn't catch sight of the burning, angry face of Victoria as she brought over the boiling water and stuck the nettle into it.

'Are you thinking of making the tea this century?' sniped the witch from the other side of the paper.

For a moment Tansy and Joey were afraid Victoria was about to throw the liquid over Petunia. Then, picking up the cup and saucer as if they were of the very finest china (instead of cracked earthenware with the handle missing), she handed them to the witch, asking sweetly, 'Sugar?'

'Of course not,' snapped back the witch, diving again behind the newspaper.

The children winked at each other. Maybe . . .

'Zounds!' shouted the witch suddenly, poking the newspaper on the back page with a long bony finger. 'That Ivy ffrench-Fawcett is at it again!'

'Ivy ffrench-Fawcett?' chorused the children.

'Yes . . . yes . . . that's what I said,' scoffed Petunia, searching for a stronger light to read the headline again. Squinting closely at the paper, she read out in a derisive voice, 'Miss Ivy ffrench-Fawcett, the concerned and caring witch, has undertaken to raise £5,000 for the local charity fund. A coffee morning will be held in Creaky Hall this Saturday to decide on upcoming events. Everyone is invited to attend to promote this worthy cause. . .

'Hah! What next? Miss Ivy ffrench-Fawcett . . . for the Nobel Peace Prize! Miss Ivy ffrench-Fawcett . . . for President! Bah!'

Furball slid into the nearest armchair. Whenever PP started to talk about Ivy ffrench-Fawcett, her biggest rival in Knockaleen, he felt the need of a stout chair. The children, looking at the photograph in the paper, saw a rather plump jolly-faced woman dressed in a large floppy hat and a large flower-printed dress; she carried a bulky straw basket.

Miss Ivy ffrench-Fawcett was clever and witty and very good at witchcraft, whereas PP just couldn't get her act together. Why, she couldn't even ... Furball didn't like to think about it, it was so awful! Not that she ever talked about *it* but there were some things that a witch's cat knows without telling.

Just reading about Miss Jolly ffrench-Fawcett was enough to cause Petunia to dance around in a rage. Tripping over Tansy, she snapped, 'Stop cluttering up the floor, pest!'

Tansy burst into tears and the witch fixed her with a gimlet eye. Suddenly a strange feeling of nostalgia filled the room.

'YOU!' shouted PP, pointing a finger at the shrinking child.

Everyone was quite unprepared for what happened next. Some dim cloud of memory stirred in Tansy's brain. Standing up as straight as if she had a ramrod through her spine, she clasped her hands behind her back and, looking into the far distance, began to intone in a high shrill voice:

THE ANIMALS' ALPHABET

The ant is really rather dull,
He works by night and day.
I know the Bible thinks he's great,
But I wish he'd learn to play!

The polar bear loves snow and ice,
His coat is thick and white.
And if I'm naughty in the day,
He'll get me in the night!

The crocodile is mainly teeth,
But when he smiles – beware!
He simply wants to snap you up,
And drag you to his lair!

Tansy paused (there were twenty-six verses in the poem), but before she could take breath and continue Petunia made a strange gurgling sound.

'Beautiful!' She sounded completely overcome. 'That was beautiful! I haven't heard such beautiful poetry since I was a girl.' A faraway look came into her eye as she remembered, 'My sister Tullalah and I used to recite poetry together. Such wonderful evenings we used to have at Creaky Hall ... before ...' her voice broke, 'before ... those nasty ffrench-Fawcetts...' She was unable to continue; even Furball felt affected.

Petunia peered closely at Tansy. She pinched her

cheeks. She ruffled her hair. Tansy didn't dare to breathe; she felt sure the witch was measuring her for the big old stewpot on the top of the stove. She screwed her eyes tight and waited to hear the worst . . .

'You, Tansy!' gushed the witch delightedly. 'You are to be dressed in the finest silks and satins and you mustn't work at all. You remind me of myself as a child. I was just like you. . .'

'I do? I am?' gasped Tansy, carefully opening one eye, as Victoria, Joey and Furball stared in disbelief.

'Yes, I could grow quite used to you on account of your face being so familiar,' mused Petunia. 'You shall just sit on silken cushions and quote poetry. And I will look at you and remember what a beautiful child I used to be . . .'

She sat down suddenly and her mood changed. Pointing at Virginia and Joey she screamed, 'As for you two! From now on, you'll cook and wash and clean and scrub and . . . and . . .' She couldn't think of what else there was to do as she had never been over-partial to housework. 'And I don't want to hear a sound or a squeak out of you. Just get on with the work and keep out of my way.'

Closing her eyes she dropped off to sleep muttering, 'You, Vapona, find yourself a corner in the attic . . . and, Joey, you can sleep under the dining-room table in case of burglars.'

'Anyone,' thought Furball, 'anyone who'd burgle this place would have to have birds' eggs for brains!'

4

Meeting at Creaky Hall

Saturday morning dawned warm and sunny in Dockleaf Cottage. The witch lay fast asleep under her enormous black satin quilt, dreaming, no doubt, of ways to outsmart Ivy ffrench-Fawcett.

In her chintzy little bedroom, Tansy lay on scented sheets, wearing rather splendid pyjamas with a large letter P on the pocket. The witch had 'found' them somewhere.

Up in the dusty wooden attic, Victoria slept on what felt like a rather lumpy straw pallet, between old trunks and odd-shaped boxes. She didn't know where Joey had ended up — Petunia had ordered him out of the dining-room as she said he might damage the carpet; probably in the coal-house.

It seemed to Victoria that she had only just fallen asleep before she woke to the sound of a shrill voice floating upstairs.

'Lazybones!' it shouted. 'Get up at once! Get down here! You know I have to be at the meeting in Creaky Hall by eleven.'

Victoria hurried downstairs. The witch and Tansy were already sitting at the table and she nearly choked with rage as she set fresh blackberry juice and wafer-thin toast before them.

'Just you wait!' she hissed under her breath as she passed Tansy, who eyed her nervously and seemed to lose her appetite. Not that PP had much time to eat either; she was too busy shouting instructions at Joey.

'Fill the coal scuttle. Light the fire. No, don't — it's too hot. Sweep the hall. Polish the brasses. Open the window. Shut the window...'

As Joey dropped whatever he was doing to obey the next instruction, very little actually got done. However, the witch, who was scurrying around like an angry bluebottle, hardly seemed to notice.

'Look at the time! I'm late...'

They all looked. But there was no clock anywhere.

'Furball, where's the clock?' she screamed. 'What an idiot! If you ever did have a brain, Tatty, it must have been stolen.'

The little cat shook his head resignedly. He was used to the witch's sharp tongue. He watched her as she tried in vain to tell the time from a big brass sundial *inside* the house.

'I'll be late ... I'll be late...' moaned the witch, grabbing her outdoor things. 'If only ... if only ...' Just as she was about to dash out through the door, she stopped and a cunning look came into her eyes.

'Now, listen, you pesky pests. Nobody is to come to the door, or go to the window. You're all to stay here, eyes shut tight, for the next ten minutes and nobody is to look out. Get it?'

'Why doesn't she fly?' said Victoria. 'I thought all witches flew about on broomsticks.'

Furball looked at her sadly as she went on, 'What a silly stupid creature. However, we won't be here for ever. We'll make plans . . . and escape!'

Furball's ears pricked up at the mention of his favourite word 'escape'. Oh . . . to escape!

Nevertheless, they were all careful, including Furball, to keep their eyes tightly closed. The minutes passed. Suddenly they heard an enormous crash as if someone had fallen heavily. They rushed to the window and — surprise, surprise — there was Petunia, who should have been half-way to Creaky Hall by now, limping down the road at a furious gallop.

As they stared after her in wonder, a head appeared over the paintless gate.

'Hi!' shouted the head under a peaked cap. 'Parcel here for Miss P. Pennefeather. Will somebody sign?'

'Another do-it-yourself kit,' thought Furball and his heart sank. What would it be this time? Callisthenics for Coven Cats?

As the children rushed over, delighted to see a new face, the man chuckled.

'Going to the fancy-dress, are you? Those clothes look like real antiques. My boy's going as The Mad Hatter.'

'Going to what?' asked Joey, before Victoria interrupted him quickly.

'Yes, yes! That's right. We're going to take part in the fancy-dress competition. We'll soon be on our way.'

'Oh,' said the head, reappearing. 'Tell Miss Pennefeather I'm not coming up this lane again until she does something about those potholes. Danger money . . . that's what you'd need to come up here . . .

danger money,' and he disappeared off down the lane, painfully weaving a path through the holes.

'Well, that's put it in a nutshell,' said Virginia. 'We can't go round in these old-fashioned clothes any more. We'd better ask for some new ones before we become the joke of the neighbourhood ... and I for one,' she went on haughtily, 'will not be laughed at.'

'Perhaps when she gets back from the meeting she'll be in a good mood,' said Joey.

'I wouldn't count on it,' thought Furball, 'I wouldn't count on it at all.'

By the time Petunia arrived at Creaky Hall she was all hot and bothered from the furious running. Sinking heavily into a seat at the back of the hall, which was absolutely packed, she squinted up towards the dais.

A tall thin woman, Mrs. Daphne Furey, was complimenting Miss Ivy ffrench-Fawcett from under a large straw hat on her 'outstanding support in raising funds for the roof of the local hospital', and she continued in a cajoling voice, 'I call on everyone to give their time and support willingly to her latest project. Ladies and gentlemen, I give you ... Miss Ivy ffrench-Fawcett.'

The clapping and cheering went on for some minutes before Petunia's hated rival stood up in her very sensible flat shoes. Beaming brightly, she waved at everyone until she finally came to a halt at the grey ringlets in the very back row.

'Ladies and gentlemen, it is indeed an honour for me to be with you again on another fund-raising mission,' she boomed loudly. 'As you know we are all undertaking various tasks to raise money to buy reference books for the local Historical Society. They

are all listed here on the board at the top of the room. Anyone who hasn't already picked one should do so now. And as you do, cross it off the list.'

There was an immediate stampede and by the time Petunia got to the board all the items had been crossed out — except one. A dinner party! Coffee mornings, garden tours, art lessons, cake sales — all had been chosen and had great big blue lines scratched through them. PP scowled blackly and hissed, 'Snooks and air-pockets! Only a dinner party left.' She thought of the organisation, the time, the trouble, and she hesitated.

'Well, of course . . .' the voice of Ivy ffrench-Fawcett, who had crept up behind her, was full of honied sympathy. 'If it's beyond you to cook a little food and receive a few friends in your quaint little home. . .'

Petunia's lower lip turned black and wrinkled as Miss Ivy continued, 'I could, of course, ask my great-great-great-aunt Savage, who's blind in one eye and wears glasses in the other. She'd be only too dee-lighted. . .'

'Of course I can do it,' the cornered Petunia choked in rage. She and Ivy had been at school together. Now Ivy seemed to outshine her at everything.

'Righteeho!' went on Miss ffrench-Fawcett, enjoying herself. 'Shall we say next Saturday for the dinner party?'

'What time shall we be there?' enquired Daphne Furey. 'I have *thousands* of arrangements to make.'

'Dinner at eight!' snapped Petunia.

Everyone agreed and the meeting ended. It would seem that Ivy ffrench-Fawcett had outsmarted Petunia once again. . .

5

The Terrible Secret

Meanwhile, back at Dockleaf, the Great Clean-up had just started. But Victoria's idea of directing while the others slaved wasn't quite working out.

After breakfast Tansy retired to the parlour where she reclined on a silk-cushioned chair, a box of Petunia's best *pralines* at her side. She turned a sulky ear to all Victoria's threats and blandishments.

'Petunia wouldn't like it,' she said. 'She told me to sit here and do nothing except think of more poetry for her. Anyway, I'd ruin my dress,' she reached out a languid hand for another chocolate, 'and my hands would get quite coarse. Besides the place is full of spiders . . . and I'm terrified of spiders. And it's all so dirty. I don't think it *could* be cleaned.' She looked at Victoria's furious face and added '. . .Miss.'

'Well, I'm not going to live in a dirty house. I don't know how you can. Where's your moral fibre?' Registering a distinct lack of moral fibre, Victoria left with a few parting shots. 'I hope you come out in spots, that you get a pain in all corners of your tummy and end up with spiders crawling all over you.

'Poetry, huh! Don't forget *How doth the lazy little drone?* . . . and don't call me "Miss". We're all equal here. Only,' as she slammed the door, 'some of us seem to be more equal than others!'

Joey was willing to do anything . . . the question was *could* he do anything? When she put him to cleaning the windows he broke a pane of glass and it took all her dexterity to put it back together again. When he tried to scrub the kitchen floor, he knocked over the bucket of water and it took them an age to mop it up. And when he polished the brasses, he left green smudges all over the place.

Part of the trouble was that he just didn't seem to see dirt. He gave the oven a cat's lick and pronounced it perfect, and grime-encrusted saucepans and pans seemed perfectly normal to him. Victoria shuddered and tried not to think of his lifestyle.

'What *can* you do?' she asked at length.

'Horses, Miss!' he grinned. 'I'm very good with the horses. Why,' he went on proudly, 'tis said I could coax a horse to jump Galway Bay.'

But there were, alas, no horses at Dockleaf Cottage. She finally decided to use him to fetch and carry, starting with the family of frogs which he relocated in the garden pond.

She assessed her team of two. Tansy, probably able but distinctly unwilling; Joey willing but distinctly unable.

Down on her hands and knees scrubbing the floor, using a cloth with holes in it and a brush with half the bristles missing, she thought of the irony of her, Victoria, cherished only daughter of Sir Basil Ross-O'Brien, Bt., doing work that an under-kitchenmaid wouldn't and a stable-boy couldn't do. She gritted her teeth and reminded herself of her ancestors who had built empires in India and Africa with, possibly, less promising material.

She would soon lick that pair into shape. Or her name wasn't the Hon. Victoria Elena Ross-O'Brien.

'If only ... if only ...' thought Petunia as she hurried

home. 'If only ... I'd show them ...' she muttered furiously all the way.

She flounced into the house, ignoring the children, and made straight for her bedroom. Flinging herself down on the creaking springs she reached under the pillows, pulled out a large well-used book and began reading it intently.

Joey, sent up by Victoria to ask were there any more cleaning materials, came back and reported she was reading a book.

'A book?'

And sure enough, when Victoria went up and had a look through the keyhole, she could see that the witch *was* reading a book — a book called *Flight Training for Pilots!* She was reading it very carefully indeed, and

seemed to shut it every few minutes and mutter aloud before opening it again.

'The way people do who are trying to learn off nine times nine,' thought Victoria, a little puzzled.

Furball, who had followed them upstairs, pawed Victoria's leg as if to say, 'Follow me.'

Leading them both quietly out of the house, they crept around the back and down the garden to an old wooden shed that was almost hidden under a giant apple tree.

Joey struggled with the door but could not open it.

'Locked!' he reported.

But Victoria was already round at the side. 'Look, there's a small window. Perhaps we can see what's inside. Give me a leg up.' She climbed the lower branch

of the apple tree and peered in through the grimy window.

'Unbelievable!' she gasped. 'Utterly unbelievable! It's full of . . .'

Suddenly the witch appeared and shouted at them, 'You lot, what do you think you're doing, looking in at my shed.'

'We thought . . . we thought it needed cleaning,' said Victoria coolly.

'Don't touch it!' snapped the witch.

'Why do you need so many broomsticks?' Victoria, though faltering a little under the witch's glare, couldn't help asking the question.

'Snooks and jet-lag, what business is it of yours?' snapped the witch, aiming a kick at poor Furball. 'Well . . .' she paused for a moment, 'since you know what's in there, Miss Busybody, you may as well know it all. I've forgotten how to fly!' she said bitterly.

She threw open the door of the shed and the children gasped — it was full almost to the roof of broken and crushed broomsticks! There were cracked ones, splintered ones, frontless ones, backless ones, squashed ones and blunted ones! Broomsticks with plasters and bandages! Broomsticks with L-plates! Broomsticks with red flags for danger! Broomsticks of all shapes and sizes and conditions . . . but not one intact . . . not a single one undamaged . . .

'So *that's* what the crash was this morning,' thought Victoria, 'and why we weren't to look out . . . she tried to fly to Creaky Hall and crashed!' Aloud, she said to Petunia. 'But I thought all witches knew how to fly the day they were born?'

'Well, I just forgot,' snapped the witch, banging the door shut and locking it again. Whooshing the two children up the garden in front of her, she grumbled aloud, 'Old Ivyleaf wouldn't be head witch for long . . . if only I could fly . . . if only I could fly . . .'

When they got back to the house, Tansy rushed out to find out what had happened.

'You missed all the excitement,' said Victoria mysteriously. 'But don't let's keep you from the parlour.'

'Oh, Miss,' said poor Tansy. 'I'd rather be with you. It's no fun in the parlour all by myself.'

The older girl put her arm around Tansy and led her down the hall. 'Don't worry,' said Victoria gracefully, 'I'll allow you to help from now on.'

6

Another Battle of Wits

The meeting at Creaky Hall and the finding of the flightless broomsticks had put Petunia into such a foul temper that it was two days before Victoria thought the time ripe to mention new clothes.

The witch had flung herself into a chair by the stove, where she sat glaring and grinding her gums.

'It's bad enough when she grinds endlessly,' fumed Furball, 'but glaring and grinding! Probably got the idea from one of her do-it-yourself kits that she keeps sending off for.'

Flanked by Tansy and Joey, Victoria cleared her throat. 'Ahem, Petu ... I mean Miss Witch ... do you suppose we might have some clothes? I mean, these are over a hundred years old ... and even the postman thought we were in fancy dress...'

She quailed under the beadiness of the witch's eye.

'New clothes! New clothes!' scoffed Petunia. 'What an idea. When did I last get new clothes? Answer me that, brat!'

Turning fondly to Tansy, she purred, 'Well, there's nothing wrong with *your* dress, dear. Wore it myself. Pure silk satin. Always was the belle of the ball. Everyone called me such a winsome child...' she mused dreamily, before grabbing Victoria and giving her grubby dress a close inspection. Then, releasing her smartly, she peered at Joey's torn shirt.

'Just needs an odd stitch here and there with a waxed pig's bristle, that's all. New clothes, indeed!'

'Oh, please look,' pleaded Victoria, holding up her dress, 'this part's got no pattern left on.'

'Hmmm,' agreed the witch. 'It *does* seem to be a bit the worse for wear, on the outside.'

'And my shirt is in giblets,' added Joey.

'Hmmm,' and 'Haaa,' muttered Petunia, grinding furiously as she paused in front of the stove. Tripping over Furball, she gleamed wickedly, 'Snooks and wingspans ... your clothes are only worn and faded on the OUTSIDE.'

'Ye-es,' agreed Victoria, 'but ...'

'But all clothes have two sides! Turn them INSIDE OUT, dingbats!'

As she hurried off to her bedroom, gurgling at her own wit, she threw a parting shot over her bony shoulder. 'Parachute silk. Plenty of parachute silk left over since the late 1940s — nobody wanted it after the war. Make clothes out of that, you pests.'

The children stared at the bale of old orange parachute silk that the witch had pulled out of the airing cupboard by the stove.

'Maybe ... I mean, it's not too cold now in the summer ... maybe ...' Tansy's voice trailed away as she saw Victoria's grim face.

'Listen, you pair of bird-brains. I'm not going around in hundred-year-old clothes *or* in fifty-year-old moth-eaten parachute silk. I'm going to get some really modern clothes and make that old witch pay for them...'

'That's it,' shouted Joey excitedly. 'We'll take her money — I bet she keeps it in one of the potholes by the gate.'

'You may be right,' said Victoria. 'I've never seen her with a reticule, so she doesn't carry money around with her.'

'What's a reti ... a retic...?' Tansy asked in a puzzled voice.

'It's an old-fashioned drawstring coin-purse, bird-brain,' Victoria answered knowledgeably.

The children crept out through the front door, taking great care not to bang it, and began searching in the pot-holes for notes or coins.

A little later, tired and dusty, Victoria sighed sadly, 'It's no use. Witches musn't have money.'

'Come to think of it,' chirped Tansy, 'you never hear money mentioned in any witch's story...'

'That's right, pesky pests,' roared Petunia, sticking

her head out of the kitchen window. 'Witches never carry coins. Ruins their balance on take-off.'

'Well, that shouldn't worry you...' whispered Victoria to the others, who grinned hugely at the joke.

The grinning annoyed PP greatly and she raged, 'Get back in here, at once. My shoes need polishing. All 300 pairs of them. Look smart!'

The three of them trooped indoors, and up to Petunia's room. Victoria paced about in front of the witch's huge chest of drawers, which had DANGER signs marked on every drawer.

'Listen,' she said practically. 'The witch *must* pay for things. I mean, she sends off for endless do-it-yourself kits. If she doesn't carry money, she pays in another way. Look at what I found in the evening paper yesterday.' She pulled a piece of paper out of her pocket and Tansy and Joey crowded around to see. It was headed 'BANKING SERVICES'.

Victoria read out the paragraph heads, 'Savings Accounts ... Deposit Accounts ... Credit Cards ...'

'What's credit cards?' asked Tansy.

'Look, it shows one here. It's a small card with your name and number on it. When you want to buy something, you use it instead of money. And the bank sends you the bill later! Old Petunia must have a savings-account book ... or a piggy bank ... or a credit card...'

Silent and solemn, the three children stood and stared at the drawers, wondering what danger they contained. Then Victoria stepped forward smartly and tugged open the cluttered drawers, while Tansy and Joey held their breaths. Nothing happened!

'Of all the confidence tricks,' said Victoria in disgust. 'Come on, let's make a thorough search.'

And in the witch's drawers they found bundles of letters tied up with pink ribbon, holiday brochures ('Fly to the Faraway Caribbean'), sealing wax, luggage labels marked 'Fragile' and 'This Side Up', ancient recordings of *Madame Butterfly* (with 'fly' heavily underlined), gramophone needles, boot-laces, plastic spoons, hallowe'en catalogues with such titles as *How to Hob and Nob*, old-fashioned fountain pens, torn-off corners of envelopes with unfranked stamps, sheet music in endless variety for such songs as *Come Fly with Me*, *Higher and Higher*, and *If I were a Rich Witch*, nine hundred and ninety-nine 'Final Demands' for Income Tax, Supertax, Surtax, Levies and Health Contributions, appeal forms, old driving-licences, fire insurance policies, leaflets and booklets on such topics as *Weight-Watching for Witches*, *How to Become a Witch of Substance*, *Easy Recipes for the Career Witch*, *The*

Witch's Herbalist, Draught-Proofing for Enchanted Homes ... and dozens and dozens of do-it-yourself kits...

The witch had a keen interest in new inventions; she was always reading the small ads section in the newspapers and sending off for the kits. There had been so many brilliant ideas, remembered Furball: Teach Yourself Hang-Gliding off the Stairs, Do-it-Yourself Dynamite, Home-made Fireworks in Ten Easy Lessons, How to Read Crystal Balls for the Short-sighted, Build your own Aircraft in 20,000 Easy Pieces, Childhood Medicines and Cures to Investigate and Enjoy, How to Grow your own Teeth from Seed ...

'Hmm,' sniffed Furball ruefully. 'It all comes back to me now — as my uncle the skunk said when the wind changed.' If the truth were known, he had suffered deeply through having to take part in all Petunia's experiments as her 'laboratory' assistant. Pawing what was left of his whiskers after the Fireworks Kit, Furball again thought with longing of escape.

But in all the mountains of junk the children unearthed, there was not one single deposit book, piggy bank or credit card to be seen.

'What a waste of time!' thought Victoria crossly. She was just putting back The Fail-Safe Method of Broomstick Management when she noticed Tansy looking at her with horror in her eyes. Or rather beyond her to the open door.

The witch had just appeared in the room.

'Snooping again, Missy?' she sneered. 'And how many pairs of shoes have you polished?'

She flung open a giant old wooden cabinet which stretched from floor to ceiling. It was jammed full of black and grey point-toed shoes.

'We'll do them immediately,' promised Victoria, beginning to pile the shoes in a neat row.

'No, not them. You ... Vapours!' ordered the witch, tossing all the shoes into a big heap.

'Now, look here,' grumbled Victoria. 'You've gone and mixed them all up. I'll have to pair them up again.'

'That's the idea,' snarled the witch, 'twice the fun!' Pointing to the other two children, she said, 'It's time for the froglets' swimming lesson.' Throwing back the shower curtain, she screamed, 'I've been robbed ... where are they?'

'In the pool,' faltered Joey.

'They slipped out there last night,' put in Tansy.

'Then go out there after them. They'll drown ... Here, take their swimming report with you. Now — look sharp.'

They all disappeared, leaving Victoria in the shadow of the mountain of point-toed shoes.

7

New Clothes for Old

Later in the evening, Tansy and Joey came back to the kitchen where the witch was sitting in her ball-of-string chair. She seemed in high good humour as she sipped her widow's port.

'And how are my amphibians? Did they do their flips and flops today?'

'Oh, yes, beautifully,' chimed the children together. They now knew it was best to agree with the witch ALWAYS.

'I wonder where Victoria is,' whispered Tansy, as they made the witch a nice strong cup of herb tea. 'There hasn't been sight or sound of her in at least four hours.'

'I be thinking,' said Joey, 'the work has finally gone and killed her. I mean it's not as if she was reared up to it...'

'We'd better go upstairs and see ... when the witch falls asleep.'

As soon as the kitchen was filled with lots of 'zzzzzs...' the pair crept upstairs. They couldn't hear a sound and Joey, plucking at Tansy's skirt, whined, 'Oh, and another thing ... I think I'm afraid of dead bodies...' His voice melted under Tansy's fierce gaze.

'Oh, do shut up, bird-brain, and open the door.'

They opened it very quietly, fearful of what they might find.

'Is she...? Is she...?' cried Joey, with his eyes still tightly closed.

'No, idiot,' whispered Tansy. 'She's staring into a shoe.'

Flicking his left eye open he looked at Victoria who was lying on the floor, heels in the air, staring fixedly into a rather battered old shoe. 'Oh, no! She's gone and been took over by the shoe madness ... my aunt in America...'

'Oh, do shut up,' interrupted Tansy. Then running over to Victoria she scolded, 'You've only polished ten pairs of shoes. What *have* you been doing?'

'I've been thinking,' was the airy answer.

Reaching inside the shoe she pulled out a plastic card with 'Miss Petunia Pennefeather' and the number 55555 on it.

'Look!' she said excitedly. 'It's a credit card. The witch must carry her belongings in her shoes when she's flying.'

'When she's what?'

'Well, when she's travelling,' corrected Victoria. 'Now, amn't I brilliant? This little piece of plastic card will get us all the new clothes we want!'

Their hearts lifted at the thought until Joey said dubiously, 'Sure, neither of you would ever pass for Miss PP herself ... not as if she'd pass for an ordinary person with them ringlets and all...'

'I've thought of that,' smiled Victoria smugly. 'Which is why we're going to order our clothes by phone, using Petunia's credit card number.'

'Oh, please, please ... can I have some clothes like the girl on the front page last night,' begged Tansy.

'I don't know what size I am,' wailed Joey.

'Not to worry! I'm a big size. Tansy, you're a small size, and Joey is ... in between ...' guessed Victoria. 'Now both of you make sure you keep old Puttyface busy in the morning so I can use the phone.'

'But . . . she'll notice the new clothes,' groaned Tansy, struck by a sudden thought.

'Not her! Not with her poor eyesight,' said Victoria.

The next morning the witch made Tansy help her with flight study. She would recite all the proper terms, 'Lift-off', 'Set-down', 'Slip-stream' etc. etc., and Tansy would remind her of the ones she always left out.

'All clear,' whispered Joey, keeping a look-out between the bedroom and the hall while Victoria ordered the clothes.

Replacing the phone, she smiled, 'They'll be here on Friday, so make certain one of us gets to the postman before old PP.'

On Friday, everything went according to plan and the children nabbed the postman in time. The clothes fitted perfectly, except for the jeans which they rolled up anyway. Tansy put lots of bright combs and bobbles in her hair, and Joey decided to wear his shirt tails outside his jeans.

The children felt really happy for the first time in ages and whooped about in their brand-new runners, gyrating to the pop music on the witch's antique wireless.

'I'm Vicki from now on,' sang Victoria. 'Victoria — what a name! Old-fashioned and prissy . . .'

'Listen to this,' giggled Tansy. 'I've just made it up. Do you think old PP will like it?'

Witches are born in cobwebs and dust,
Even their rattlers are covered in rust.
They don't learn spelling or sums – only worse,
Just how to bewitch and be spellbound – and curse!

They fell about laughing at the silliness of it, when a loud yell pierced their eardrums.

'Hah, snooking air-pockets, what's all the din about?'

The witch scurried into the kitchen, and the children held their breath. What if she noticed . . .

'Just a minute, Missy!' she menaced towards Victoria. 'Just a little spooky minute.'

The children stood as still as statues. Perhaps her eyesight wasn't as bad as they supposed.

'Yes, Miss Witch?' faltered Vicky. 'Is anything the matter?'

'Of course it is, and you all know very well what it is. . .'

'I . . . we do. . .' she quailed. She could see Joey's eyes bulging.

'Yes. . . . You know perfectly well I only put on the wireless on the first Friday, every hundred years — and this is *not* it. Pests!' she bellowed, snapping the cord out of the socket and flouncing back to her studies.

The children collapsed in a heap of relieved giggles as the mutterings of the witch came through the door.

'Pop music. Porridge between the ears. Porridge between the ears . . . Grrr . . .'

8
Spooked!

The next few days in the witch's cottage were some of the busiest Furball could ever remember. Though the cottage was now reasonably clean, it was amazing all the work that had still to be done. PP hadn't given a dinner party for at least twenty years so no one quite knew where to start. A set of matching chairs had to be assembled. Serving dishes were rescued from behind doors where they were doubling as doorstops. Knives and forks couldn't be found anywhere at first, until at last they were discovered in baize-lined mahogany boxes in the attic. China had to be carefully washed; there wasn't of course a complete set of anything but Vicki got round that difficulty by using different patterns for the different courses. Glasses were a problem; there were only cracked oddments until Joey found a whole box of cut crystal which had never even been opened.

So the children cleaned and swept, and swept and polished. Furball dusted the high corners with his long tail, Tansy shone the small window panes until the light actually came through, and when Vicki substituted soft but bright table lamps (from PP's bedroom) for the 40-watt overhead bulbs that threw a funereal gloom, the parlour and dining-room seemed quite cosy and cheerful.

Joey, using an old charcoal stick, had drawn great big curly moustaches on all the gentlemen with the pained expressions hanging in the parlour. It didn't exactly improve the gentlemen, but it took the very gloomy look off the walls. Even Vicky, who knew that one Must Never Meddle with Antiques, had to admit it was a big improvement.

'I really don't know HOW she would have managed without us,' said Vicky, as she surveyed the scene on the day of the dinner party. The table had been set and a large bowl of PP's favourite flowers (stinging nettles and dandelions) had been placed between five large grey candles. Five of everything was sure to please the witch as five was her favourite number.

The children still didn't know what the guests were going to get to eat. Petunia had locked herself into the kitchen for an hour that morning, then announced everything was ready.

'Maybe she *can* produce magic food,' thought Vicky.

'Ha!' chortled the witch as she swept downstairs that afternoon in a hideous black taffeta dress and a cloak

printed with bats and lined with scarlet. As she looked about the dining-room, her half-moon earrings jangling, she seemed in high good spirits.

'Who are the guests?' asked Vicky. Seeing the witch was about to shout at her, she went on quickly, 'I mean we should have place-cards. . .'

'Place-cards?' echoed PP.

'. . . so that everyone knows where to sit.'

'What a splendid idea!' purred the witch. 'That'll stop them in their tracks.'

'Now, who do we have?' she mused. 'Old ffrench-Fawcett, of course . . . two small ffs . . . never could spell, that family. Sir Lucius O'Looney . . . pompous old toad . . . not all there. Mrs. Daphne Furey . . . hell had no fury like a Furey scorned. Mr. Timothy Ignatius Norman Kettle . . . named for all his rich uncles . . . ends up as Mr. Tin Kettle. Mr. Woulfe and Miss Lambe . . . always go everywhere together . . . you should hear them,' she adopted a mincing voice, '"We're the wolf and the lamb" . . . passes as a joke for the first 500 times. And finally Mr. McAdoo . . . much ado about nothing. . .'

'Eight, with you,' counted Vicky. 'Will there be enough to eat . . . I mean, what is there to eat?'

'Snails and nettles,' snapped the witch. 'Good enough for them. I'll settle old fiddle-faddle and her cronies once and for all . . . Now for Spell 208. . .'

She rushed into the kitchen, followed by the children, and started lashing large dollops from various bottles and jars into a mixing bowl.

'Spook Cocktail,' she giggled, squinting at the recipe book; she was not wearing her glasses as she was in her party best.

'What's that?' asked Tansy.

'Mind your own business,' snapped PP. But as there's no point in being so very clever unless everyone knows about it, she explained, 'One glass of this and you're spooked! When they drink a glass of this nice absolutely awful cocktail they won't be able to eat a thing. All we have to do is serve the snails . . . that'll finish them. And I'll finish the left-overs tomorrow.' Petunia was very fond of snails.

'I have the funniest feeling. . .' thought Furball.

So did Vicky. 'Well, at least there's plenty of brown bread,' she said, being now a very fair hand at home-made brown bread. 'I'll make an extra batch. . .'

At exactly 7.30 pm, the big old bell outside Dockleaf Cottage pealed. It wasn't an ordinary door-bell (well, was there ever anything ordinary in or around Dockleaf Cottage?). It was, in fact, a ship's bell that old Saltypaws had brought back home after one of his voyages.

Tansy ushered everyone in, dropping a curtesy as she did so. 'What a charming child,' thought everyone, as they were shown into the parlour, where they sat wheezing on and on about this and that.

Last to arrive, making her usual royal entrance, came Miss Ivy ffrench-Fawcett, escorted by Sir Lucius O'Looney.

'Am I the last?' she simpered. 'Soo sorry to have kept everybody waiting.'

'Well, you didn't keep *me* waiting,' sniffed Petunia, who waited until they were all seated, then had herself specially announced by Tansy, before sweeping in wafting clouds of old-fashioned lavender scent and mothballs.

Everyone was looking around in apprehension, fearing the worst — and, as everyone know, the worst could so easily happen in Dockleaf Cottage.

'Petunia, dear,' said Ivy sweetly. 'Petunia, dear, do you suppose one could have a little something...' She looked expectantly around, twiddling her endless string of pearls. 'I mean, one works up a jolly good thirst hacking a way through a jungle to get here, ha, ha...'

Everyone laughed at that, until Petunia pointed to Joey and said in her sweetest posh voice, 'But, of course, dears. You can have all the Spook — I mean, fruit cocktail — you like. Boy, the tray!' And in came Joey with a trayful of gleaming crystal glasses, filled with the most deliciously coloured drink. PP peered at his dickie-bow, which Vicki had run up from an old hairnet or two, but said nothing. Without her glasses she couldn't be sure they were hers.

'How splendid!' thought everyone, taking a glass. Then they noticed Tansy who was following Joey, a collecting box in hand.

'All contributions gratefully received,' purred Petunia.

'Do you mean?' spluttered Mr. T. I. N. Kettle. 'Do you mean we have to pay you for a cocktail in your house, at a dinner party?'

His eyebrows moved up and down so fast on his forehead that they looked like car windscreen-wipers.

'You surely don't object to a ... small ... token ... gesture. For Ivy's so-deserving charity,' replied Petunia sweetly. Then deftly cornering Sir Lucius's wallet which he had just produced, she took out a couple of £50 notes. 'There, that should cover it. Boy,' she ordered, 'serve them all the Spook ... er ... fruit cocktail they can drink.'

As she left the room to put the money in a safe place, the guests talked nervously.

'Do you really suppose she can cook?' whined Daphne Furey.

'Perhaps it's going to be a frozen TV Toadleg Dinner,' whinged Miss Lambe. 'Or maybe even Black Bat Stew.'

Mr. McAdoo whispered desperately, 'Are we insured for accidents? I mean, will the insurance companies pay if it's a self-inflicted accident? Oh, if we didn't need this money so badly for a Good Cause, I'd never have been talked into it...'

Mr. Woulfe began loosening his tie, saying, 'Dear, dear, I've forgotten my indigestion pills again...'

Ivy said nothing; she only smiled — a secret smug look on her face. She was going to see 'Stupid PP' make an utter fool of herself again ... hee, hee!

Then, about half-way down their first glass, something strange happened in Dockleaf Cottage! Daphne Furey actually began to smile, Mr. Woulfe straightened his tie, Mr. McAdoo told a joke, and Miss Lambe asked, coyly, if she could have another. By the time everyone had finished that first drink, a mood of relaxed well-being was spreading from guest to guest.

Vicky, having a quick check through the keyhole, heard one voice saying to another, 'I'm *so* looking forward to dinner. I'm sure we're going to get something wonderful...'

'Jumping Johosapha,' she thought in horror. 'They haven't lost their appetites ... and there's nothing to eat!'

'I could have told you,' yawned Furball, who had decided to have a small pre-dinner nap. 'What she actually made was Spell 296 — How to Make People Relax and Put Them at Their Ease ... Especially Useful Before Occasions Which Might Prove Stressful — Like Dinner Parties.'

9

Dinner at Eight

For a few minutes the kitchen was in a terrible state of panic. The children ran here, there and everywhere, looking into cupboards, ransacking the fridge, even casting despairing glances at the overgrown garden.

'Stop!' yelled Vicky. 'We're behaving like hens without heads. At least we've got snails for starters ... and plenty of brown bread.'

In a flash she had marshalled her troops. 'Tansy, you go into the parlour. Keep the Spook flowing and give them a verse or two — that should do the trick.'

So in Tansy went, refilled the glasses, and dropping a low curtesy, cleared her throat and piped, 'And now I'm going to recite for you *The Animals' Alphabet*.'

'Cabaret!' said everyone. 'How dee-lightful...'

In the kitchen, Vicky said urgently to Joey, 'Now, what's in the garden?'

'Only nettles, Miss,' reported Joey.

'Nettles? Excellent! Nettle soup ... couldn't be better. Joey, go out and grab armfuls.'

'Oh, Miss ... I'll be stung to death...'

'Not if you grasp them firmly. Out!'

Tansy's voice drifted in...

> *The elephant is big and grey,*
> *I'm sure he weighs just tons.*
> *Just fancy all that massive bulk*
> *Is due to eating buns!*

'Now,' thought Vicky, 'what's in the fridge?'

There was indeed very little. Petunia had put aside a couple of brace of pigeons for *her* supper after the party (for such a bony skinny specimen she sometimes got through an astonishing amount of food — though of course she only ate every second day or so.)

Tansy was now at the letter H. . .

> *The hippo slurps and slops and slavers,*
>   *His manners are atrocious*
> *But I wouldn't care to tell him so,*
>   *Because he's quite ferocious!*

'They'll have to do,' thought Vicky. 'I'll divide them up. Joey, chop the nettles very fine and throw them into boiling water, then get me some gooseberries from the hedge beside the shed . . . oh, and a few nasturtium leaves and parsley. Quickly. . .'

What a frantic few minutes! As Vicky and Joey worked like lightning, they could hear the animal parade pass on. . .

> *The monkey swings from branch to branch,*
>   *And only pauses for his tea.*
> *How glad am I, that I am not,*
>   *A monkey in a tree!*

> *The ostrich is a splendid bird,*
>   *His legs go on for ever!*
> *But if you'd like to take one home,*
>   *You'd never catch him, never!*

'Drat the girl!' said Vicky crossly. ' She's missed out N. However, we're nearly there. Joey, pick me anything green for salad. And, Furball, do you think you could find an odd jar of cherries among the potholes? As quick as you can.'

Tansy drew a deep breath and announced verse 20.

> *The tiger snarls and claws and bites,*
> *He eats up young and old*
> *I know he'll eat me up as well,*
> *If ever I am bold!*

Just as she finished, Vicky sounded the dinner gong.

Leading the company into the dining-room, Petunia gushed, 'I'd like to say how pleezed I am that you ... that you could come and share the humble delights of my home with me! I *do* hope it will be the first of many similar little gatherings.'

Ivy was quite put out when she saw the beautifully set table, and there was much 'Oohing' and 'Ahing' over the place-cards, which Vicky had done in beautiful copperplate handwriting. The guests all put theirs in their pockets to bring home!

Petunia tinkled a tiny bell for service. Such excitement! What would it be? Then in swept Vicky with a dish of garlic-stuffed snails, piping hot.

'*Escargots!*' Sir Lucius was overwhelmed. 'I haven't tasted *escargots* since I was in Paris. Ah ... Paris in the spring ...' And away he went on the trot, telling stories of Paris and his favourite Café de Paris, where the musicians played with tiny jumper-clad monkeys on their shoulders.

'*Vive la France,*' said everyone, tucking in with gusto and replenishing their Spook.

The next course was a steaming tureen of delicately flavoured soup.

'Nettle ... with a *petit frisson* of dandelion ... and a *soupçon* of sorrel ...' Daphne Furey, always a bit of a health food nut, was practising her fractured French.

Out in the kitchen the children surveyed Vicky's masterpiece.

On each plate she had carefully placed a triangular piece of roast pidgeon. Beneath it, like waves, peeped the nasturtium leaves. To one side, halved pale green gooseberries seemed like cool mountains, above which a red cherry gave the impression of an evening sun sinking.

Tansy and Joey's eyes widened in amazement when they saw the plates.

'Wonderful!' they chorused. 'You've made a picture using the food.'

Pouring a little soured cream sauce at the bottom of each plate, Vicky sent in the servers.

'What will happen when Mr. T. I. N. Kettle sees that?' she thought. 'He's sure to be expecting meat and two veg.'

This was exactly what he had been expecting and

for a minute or two after the course was served there was a total silence. Everyone's eyes were fixed on their plates — but just as Ivy was about to give a loud howl of laughter, Mr. Woulfe exclaimed excitedly, 'Wonderful! Wonderful! *Nouvelle cuisine*!'

'It is?' faltered Ivy, her prized false teeth wobbling alarmingly. 'Nou . . . what?'

'Yes, yes!' he went on to explain. 'You see everyone's plate has a small portion of extremely tasty food, very artistically arranged.'

'How absolutely clever of you, Petunia dear,' gushed Miss Lambe, 'to organise such a healthy wholesome meal from so little.'

'Oh, you should see what I can do with the odd fish-head and half a yard of spaghetti,' scoffed Petunia, not realising they were really paying her compliments. Furball bit her ankle sharply to keep her quiet!

'Yes, we all become overweight eating huge steaks and stones of potatoes,' chipped in Daphne.

'This sort of dinner party is such a woonderful treat,' added Mr. McAdoo.

'The elderberry wine has an *extremely* fine bouquet,' sniffed Sir Lucius.

'You must give me the recipe, Petunia dear,' murmured Daphne.

'And what *super* salad!' murmured Miss Lambe, who was munching dandelions with the avidity of a rabbit.

On and on went the praise. Of the wholesome diet . . . the dangers of heart attacks . . . the perils of overeating . . . the benefits of feeling fitter.

Ivy ffrench-Fawcett, who had been about to point out the inconsistency of eating quantities of garlic butter if one wished to keep fit, decided to say nothing. She closed her mouth with a snap.

Petunia couldn't resist saying sweetly, 'How are you doing, Ivy? Soo hope you're enjoying the evening.'

The guests were now in such a good mood that when the children carried in the dessert they all clapped and cheered. Petunia (who had originally intended to frighten them!) had stuck one of her home-made fire-crackers and a tiny umbrella into each bowl of ice-cream. And when they were lit, what an exciting dessert they made, with shooting fireworks going off in every direction, like eight shooting stars around the dinner table. Luckily no one was hit — though Ivy almost had her pearl necklace severed.

'What a dinner party it has turned out to be!' thought a bewildered Furball. 'Why is it that when she wants something to turn out well, it turns out badly ... and when she wants something to turn out badly, it does just the opposite.' Shaking his head as he lurked behind the heavy old red velvet curtains he couldn't help

thinking, 'Old PP has stolen a march on old Fiddle-Faddle this time and no mistake.'

Just before the dinner guests left, Sir Lucius stood up, looking very jolly and red-faced. Raising a hand for silence, he began, 'Friends and dear Pennefeathered Petunia ... oops, the fruit cocktail,' he giggled. 'On behalf of my friends and myself I'd really like to thank you for a moost wonderful evening! A really exciting dinner party. I'd also like to say how much I admire your adventurous spirit in a world of boring dinners. Now I give you ... *For she's a jolly good fellow, For she's a jolly good fellow, ...*' And they all began to sing so heartily that Furball was quite blasted out from behind the curtain.

Later, the cat and the tired children dawdled in front of the big old stove nibbling 'dippins' (biscuits dipped in tea and cocoa) and sipping their milky cocoa, whispering in tired but excited voices long into the night...

'Remember when PP's earrings got caught in Sir Lucius's toupee...'

'What did you think of Tin Kettle's *Sur la Pont d'Avignon?*'

'Cracked! Should get himself a tin whistle!'

'Does Ivy FF hold the world record for opening and closing her mouth...'

'...without any sound coming out!'

'And all the fuss about those seedy-looking pearls. "A family heirloom"...'

'Some family ... some heirloom!'

'Hee hee ... hee hee ...'

Giggle ... giggle ...

10
War is Declared

For a time, life in Dockleaf Cottage was almost normal. The witch, sure she was the social success of the season, positively blossomed. While awaiting the flood of gilt-edged invitations which she knew would shortly arrive through the letterbox, she even started giving the children lectures on plants and herbs and lessons in geography on a big old-fashioned globe. The TV set was resurrected from the attic and they were actually allowed to watch it — when there was anything of an educational nature on, of course.

Tansy, who had missed quite a lot of schooling, really enjoyed these lessons and began to grow quite fond of the witch!

One evening they were all gathered around the old black and grey television (nothing in the cottage was EVER white). It was very difficult to see the picture as the screen was covered in dust. Petunia, whose eyesight was dim, tried to clean it, mistaking Furball's tail for a duster.

'Stop! Stop!' yelled Vicki. 'That's Furball's tail, PP.'

'Snooks and joysticks,' snapped the witch. 'He shouldn't leave it hanging around like that.'

The little cat crept under Tansy's apron. 'One of these days...' he whimpered quietly. 'One of these days I'll...'

He stopped suddenly as the voice on the TV set droned out the word 'Knockaleen'.

Everyone's eyes became glued to the screen.

64

The voice went on, 'Welcome to this week's programme of *Places and Faces!* Today we're in Knockaleen, and we're going to meet *all* the local celebrities! Good evening, Sir Lucius. You're one of the village's most prominent citizens. Perhaps later you'll show us around your organic farm and stables. . .'

'I wonder will we see anyone else we know,' cried Tansy excitedly. 'Oh look, there's Ivy ffrench-Fawcett . . . and there's Daphne Furey, talking about the Art Gallery. . .'

'Shh,' interrupted the witch rudely. '*I'll* be on in a minute. I don't want to miss myself!'

'But you can't be. You weren't interviewed,' chorused the children together.

'Of course I'll be on,' snapped Penny. 'I'm a Very Important Person in this village, ever since my wonderful dinner party. The hostess with the mostest!

A pioneer of nouv ... noo ... well, of niggardly dinners,' she floundered.

Furball and the children looked at one another with pained expressions. They knew the witch hadn't a clue about how a television programme is made and that she couldn't appear on the screen unless she had been filmed. Wouldn't she be cross when she found out?

The programme continued on its merry way, interviewing everyone who was anybody in the village, and a great many more who weren't. Except, of course, PP. When it finished, she thumped the TV set, sending large clouds of smoke and dust everywhere, and choked out, 'That's it! We are now AT WAR!! I declare war on Miss Fat-face Fiddlelegs. Her and her old cronies had better watch out,' scowled the witch, whose grammar tended to go to pieces under stress, shaking her ringlets ominously before flouncing out and kicking the door of the room shut.

Actually she *had* been invited to take part in the TV programme — but the invitation had never reached her. When delivering the children's clothes, the postman had finally fallen into pothole 47A and sprained his ankle. He vowed never to set foot in Dockleaf Lane again, which should be a warning to anyone else who leaves potholes lying around.

The television programme caused quite a stir in Knockaleen and at one of the Council meetings (held in Creaky Hall), Sir Lucius proposed the idea of making the village into a tourist attraction. The possibilities, he pointed out, were endless, as on and on he droned. Knockaleen — Haven for Heritage Homes ... Wrecked Nerves ... Potholing holidays ...' Everyone sniggered at that one.

'Perhaps,' he finished, 'we could end up by offering our lovely village as a picturesque location for the odd film or two. . .'

A mysterious glint shone in Ivy ffrench-Fawcett's eyes as she stood up to 'second' the idea.

'Friends,' she cooed in a sugary sweet little-girl voice. 'Such a brilliant idea of Sir Lucius's. You know, of course, there's going to be a nation-wide competition for *Garden Village of the Year*. Why shouldn't *we* win it?'

'I say, old girl!' threw in Mr. Woulfe. 'Super! I mean, we've all got rather jolly front gardens and things.'

'Well, most of us have,' smiled ffrench-Fawcett, looking straight at PP who had just arrived, late as usual, on account of her not being able to. . .

There was a strained silence as she threw herself into a chair. Everyone had been disappointed when she hadn't turned up for the television programme. Now they all thought — maybe it's true — maybe she just doesn't want to be friendly. So instead of asking her why she hadn't turned up, they all looked at the ceiling, hemmed and hawed, cleared their throats and avoided her eye. Which just goes to show that grown-ups can sometimes be just as childish as children!

This reception naturally put PP into a foul humour and seeing her face grow fat and furious, Ivy went on delightedly, trying very hard not to laugh at the sight of Petunia in such a rage. 'So it's settled, then,' she continued. 'We enter. And. . .' a fat finger was held up for added attention, 'to make sure we all take this seriously, I propose another competition — just for ourselves — a competition for the most beautiful garden in the village. *And* there's an incentive. . .'

As Petunia choked with rage, Furball, who had

cadged a lift in one of the witch's five pockets, hurriedly stuffed his paw between his teeth to keep from laughing out loud.

'Ha!' snarled Petunia to herself. 'That Ivy what's-her-name must have bats in her belfry if she supposes anyone in Knockaleen gives a hoot about gardens. Look at mine!'

'And,' went on old ffrench-Fawcett, who had really done her homework on this project, 'my good friends, the Savages, will give £1,000 to the winner . . . *and* make a television documentary on the winning garden.' She ended on a triumphant note and sat down to gasps of 'Oh to be on *Gardener's World.*'

Well, Furball couldn't believe his eyes. The people at the meeting jumped up and down with excitement and everyone praised Ivy's brilliant idea and pledged undying support.

Petunia simmered and shook so much that the cat was afraid his fur would fall out. She swept out muttering, 'Now is my chance to pay back that lot for the way they snubbed me after my wonderful dinner party! Well, I'll show them.' And she glowered and gloamed all the way home and long into the night, forming the Great Plan.

'Not alone will I do *nothing*! I'll make sure the judges don't miss it. . .'

Over the next few weeks the air around Knockaleen was filled with the sound of work. Such digging and planting! Such painting and repairing! Such sweeping and tidying! The likes of it had never been seen before. Soon the gardens of Knockaleen began to look even neater and tidier than ever, with flowerbeds in every corner.

Even PP seemed to have had a change of heart. Odd reports began to filter back to Creaky Hall that there was 'activity' at Dockleaf Cottage.

There was! Almost as soon as she got back from that fatal meeting, PP lined up the three children and, between clenched teeth, ordered them to fill in every pothole and make smooth the hills and hollows of Dockleaf Lane.

While the children toiled, PP redoubled her efforts to fly. But no matter how hard she tried to put into practice what she had learned off from the Pilot Book, it just didn't seem to work.

'It's the sight of those disgusting neat gardens full of brightly coloured flowers, that's what it is,' she muttered. If there was anything (after the sight of children) that made PP cross it was neatness. 'I really do feel ill,' she moaned one afternoon, climbing into

her string-holed chair. 'Fetch me some miserable medicine at once, Tattyfur.'

The children, who had just returned from fishing with some friends in the village, searched frantically to find the medicine. It just didn't do to let PP get into a bad temper.

Carrying it between his teeth, Furball dropped it quickly and scampered under the table.

'That was close,' he panted. 'Another second, and I'd surely have been whiskerless.'

Thinking that the witch had mellowed after her medicine, Vicky suggested, 'Now that we've done the lane, when are we going to start work on the garden?'

'Tell her that if we don't start soon, we'll have no chance of getting the prize,' whispered Tansy.

'Or being on television,' put in Joey, crossing his fingers.

'What are you hatching over there?' snapped the witch. 'Speak up!'

'It's just. . .' began Tansy bravely.

Noticing the witch grow stiff with temper, Vicky interrupted hastily, 'It's just that while you were out trying ... err ... flying your broomstick ... Daphne Furey called by and asked were we getting ready for the competiton.'

'Listen, you lot of pesky pests,' growled Petunia,

springing out of the chair. The children stepped back in fright.

'I, Petunia Pennefeather, am not planting *any* disgusting flowers or giving my fifty-year-old grass a haircut for any fat-bat Fiddleleaf.'

The children stood silently. The cat sat silently. And PP sulked silently. No one could think of anything to say...

The witch sat in her chair all evening and all the next day and the day after that. And nobody dared to say a word.

The day after that they had another visitor — Ivy ffrench-Fawcett in person.

'Just dropped by,' came the sugary tones, 'to see how you were getting along. We must all put our shoulders to the wheel and our best foot forward, mustn't we?'

As PP choked, she went on, 'You've made such a *super* job of the lane. It's really incredible ... I mean ... actually being able to *walk* up it to your dinky little cottage. Such a novelty! You'll notice I didn't fly here ... it was somehow much more exciting to walk!'

Petunia, who had been thinking furiously, had now recovered her wits.

'But, of course,' she cooed in equally sugary tones. 'We must make sure the judges can get to Dockleaf Cottage easily, mustn't we?'

'But, of course,' echoed Ivy faintly. That was just what the Committee had been afraid of. 'But what about your garden? When do you start work on that?'

'This very afternoon,' gushed PP. 'We were actually on our way into town to buy seeds and plants — when you so kindly dropped in. *Do* come again ... sometime ... in the next fifty years or so. . .'

As soon as Ivy had padded out through the front door and gone home to plant another nasty little row of begonias, the witch jumped out of her chair, almost standing on the sleeping cat's whiskers.

'Right, you lot. Now for Part Two of the Great Plan,' she crowed proudly. 'I'll plant seeds in my garden — but not just ordinary seeds. Oh no, I shall plant Special Seeds. Now, what do you think of that?'

Nobody pretended to notice anything odd about a cat, three children, a witch and a broomstick boarding a bus, but still — it wasn't a sight to be seen everyday. . .

Arriving at the seed shop in Weasel Snout Lane, Petunia became quite excited. 'Now,' she ordered, 'you lot! Choose any seeds you like ... but only seeds that sound odd and odious...'

The children were fascinated by the names.

'Look at these,' giggled Tansy. 'Dead nettle ... creeping hoosestrife ... pasture houseworth...'

'I like the sound of these,' grinned Joey. 'Oxeye daisies ... fine bent grass ... toad flax ... skunk cabbage...'

'Listen to these!' purred Vicki. 'Golden garlic, tobacco plant, milkweek, even bearded hybridiris.'

Nobody noticed the witch actually paying for the seeds, but everyone hoped that she did. She was so pleased with herself that she even bought the children an ice-cream. Well, she had actually intended to buy them one between three, but the stupid assistant ('sawdust between the ears', snapped the witch) scooped out three. They had a furious argument, but as the ice-cream had disappeared by the time they had finished, there wasn't much anyone could do about it.

'Three ice-creams?' crowed the witch, throwing down the money for one. 'Where's the evidence?'

'I wonder what kind of flowers will grow from these seeds?' asked Tansy sleepily on the homeward journey.

'Flowers,' roared the witch so loudly that the driver skidded a little. 'Flowers? Did I ever say I was planting flowers?'

On seeing their puzzled faces, she grinned hugely, muttering mysteriously, 'All's fair in hate and war!'

11

Behind the Barricades

The first thing the witch did on Monday morning was to build a huge barricade around the garden. She made the children hold up lengths of corrugated iron and old wooden doors and Joey nailed them all securely to each other. Then she ordered him to paint 'KEEP OUT' in large red paint on all sides.

Joey, on account of not being highly educated, wrote 'KIP OUT OF HEAR', and this drove the witch into a mighty rage.

'You newts! You perishing ding-dongs! Can't you spell? Well, that's it; you'll all have to go to the schoolhouse.'

As the children looked delightedly at one another, she flounced away, muttering, 'Bad enough being surrounded by children. But to be surrounded by *dumb* children! Only, of course, they're not dumb. They can talk plenty when they want to, etc. etc. etc. . .'

As the weeks passed, everyone grew more and more curious to see what was behind the barricade at Dockleaf Cottage. The whole village drifted by at one time or another: 'Just happened to be passing. . .' 'Can we offer you some bumblebee jam. . .?' 'I just must sit down for a few minutes — to tie my shoelace. . .' 'Can we interest you in ten days' subscription to *How to Make Silage and Influence Plants*?'

On fine days there was even the glint of telescopes being trained on the pinhole rust on the corrugated sheets.

But they found out NOTHING ...

The children were just as interested in what was happening behind the barricades.

'Maybe,' ventured Vicky to the witch, 'we'll win First Prize.'

'One Thousand Pounds!' Tansy and Joey had eyes like saucers.

'First Prize,' scoffed the witch who was humming *I'll Lead Them up the Garden Path* to herself, '*First Prize!* Prizes are for the prissy.'

At last the day of judgement arrived. One beautiful morning in August, the children helped the witch to remove the barricade.

They fell back in surprise. It certainly looked nothing like a garden. It was all dimpled green and shadowy cool, except for a pocket of sunshine near the gate; a wild garden almost, with split levels and twisting corners. There was hardly a patch of soil to be seen. A tall judas tree shouldered buddleia and fuchsia bushes. Bamboo rustled in the wind, its beautiful feathery foliage arching to the ground, creating an air of mystery. Grasses of every shape and size sprang up where they found room, as if to say, 'I'm here, invited or uninvited.' Tall tufts of sedge grass and delicate frothy fronds were mirrored in the cool water of the pond, and yellow waxy skunk cabbage grew around the sides.

The children stood silent in amazement. It was as if the garden had become a different land, a haven for exotic plants, bees, butterflies, tiny insects, under the tall judas tree.

But what would the judges think of it?

'We're sure to be disqualified,' thought Vicky gloomily, 'and we'll lose the village first place in *Garden Village of the Year* ... and we've no chance of that special prize ... and that will mean no hope of escape ... of ever ever being found by our long-lost relations...'

Meanwhile in the village there was an air of restless excitement. A great cheer went up when the television truck, with its outside broadcast camera, finally appeared and came to a stop.

Ivy ffrench-Fawcett snivelled and simpered to everyone about the 'very stiff competition'. As her garden had 57 varieties of flowers she felt sure she must be the winner.

The Savages, and two underlings with large clipboards, began taking notes and giving marks. At first, the splendidly neat little lawns, edged with tiny blue lobelia and white alyssum, and flowerbeds bright with red begonias, with the occasional herbaceous border of lupin and stock and phlox, brought forth admiring cries, but after fifty gardens, which all looked more or less the same, the judges grew weary.

Escorted by the ever-present Ivy ffrench-Fawcett, they collapsed into *Ye Olde Daffodil Teashoppe.*

'If I see another cute little pansy,' grumbled Mr. O'Moody, one of the scorekeepers. 'I shall go pie-eyed.'

'I know,' groaned Miss Cattigan. 'It's beginning to look like this is going to be a boring old. . .'

'Look!' gasped Mrs. Savage, stabbing the air furiously, as she looked over the neat garden at the back, to where the galloping green fronds of Petunia's garden were waving in the breeze.

'Ah. . . I must warn you,' simpered Ivy, following her gaze. 'Not everybody took this competition seriously. I'm afraid some amongst us Made No Effort. Everywhere has its own resident oddball. So if you'll just ignore that garden. . .'

But the judges weren't listening. Leaping to their collective feet, shouting 'Quick! Camera! Follow us! Follow us!' out through the door of the *Teashoppe* and down the lane they ran until they stumbled to a halt outside Petunia's haven of deep green forest.

The villagers followed at a little distance, their faces stiffly painted in disbelief. PP had certainly popped her pond this time. And all the time the Savages talked with their heads closely together, while the scorekeepers wrote furiously in their notebooks. Finally, noticing the looks of disbelief all around them, they spoke excitedly.

'You see,' they pointed to the garden. 'Its enormous charm lies in its almost neglected look. But to knowledgeable garden-lovers like ourselves, it's full of the most interesting and unusual plants.'

'Take this cape pondweed, for instance,' glowed Mr. Savage. Everyone stood and stared at the rather exotic-shaped leaves forming a vee in the pond. 'This plant...' (dramatic pause) '... was first introduced to these islands as long ago as 1788!'

Furball sniffed and looked at the witch knowingly.

Rushing eagerly across the creeping yellow anguefoil which grew down towards the pocket of sunlight, Miss Cattigan spoke reverently. 'And here we have a wonderful example of wisteria and buddelia. They grow so tastefully together. Yet no one has ever thought of planting them among quilted hosta leaves and scented climbing woodbine.'

The remarks came thick and fast.

'Such colour in a small space...'

'An air of mystery! And what imagination...'

'Such character! Such a splendid combination...'

Ivy ffrench-Fawcett's bottom jaw dropped so low that her prized false teeth fell out and slid into a tangle of stinging nettles, disturbing a family of brilliantly coloured peacock butterflies.

'My teeth! I've dropped my lucky tooth!' screamed Fiddleleaf. 'My priceless antique-tooth left to me by my great-great-grandwitch in her Will. I'm doomed if I don't find it.'

Everyone, seeing the witch's distraught state, agreed to look for it. Alas, it had disappeared.

'We'll have a hunt for it in the autumn,' promised PP sweetly, 'when we're clearing out the rubbish.'

'Is this is, Miss Ivy.'

Joey, who had long since mastered the art of grasping stinging nettles with ease, held up a rather yellowed tooth on the end of a tiny piece of brass wire.

'Give it to me!' said Ivy sharply, before she remembered to resume simpering. Maybe now her luck would come back and these stupid Savages would see the 'garden' for what it really was, just a load of weeds.

But the judges were discovering fresh treasures.

'Gather round, ladies and gentlemen,' whispered Mr. Savage, barely able to talk with emotion. 'This is indeed a rare sight!'

'What could he have found?' thought Furball.

Everyone peered into a mass of crinkled greenery and there, resting delicately on a strand of milkweed, was a magnificent bright orange and brown-veined butterfly.

'It's the Monarch!' whispered Mr. Savage reverently. 'It's a large American butterly, very uncommon in this country — because,' he beamed at everyone, 'the plant food it needs is that plant,' and he pointed to the milkweed. 'No caterpillars have ever been found in these parts since records began. In fact, the Monarch probably came here in the hold of a ship.' How everyone gasped at that. 'It has never been seen flying across the Atlantic, yet it can land on the water to rest, and then fly off again.'

'What a beauty,' put in Miss Savage. 'Its wings must be nearly 10cm across.'

'Probably came in one of my do-it-yourself kits from America,' mused Petunia. 'I wondered at those creepy-crawling things in the bottom of the box before the ... er ... explosion ...'

'And look,' screamed Mr. O'Moody so loudly that everyone jumped backwards, convinced that he'd seen a snake. Then his voice dropped to an awed croak. 'Look . . . the Natterjack Toad!'

'The frogs we taught swimming to,' whispered Tansy.

'I thought they looked rather palaeozoic,' contributed PP, 'that's why I took them in.'

Luckily no one heard her as they were all too busy admiring the pre-historic toads, so she kept her new-found reputation as The Great Naturalist intact.

After that the garden seemed to bewitch and charm everyone. The men admired the different kinds of foliage. The ladies marvelled at the exotic herbs and ground-cover plants. The children were fascinated by the number of insects that flew and buzzed and crawled about in the green creeping carpet.

At last, Mr. Savage, calling for 'Silence', climbed on to a nearby tree stump.

'Ladies and Gentlemen,' he began. 'We would like to congratulate you all on your fine efforts for this competition. Some of the gardens were the tidiest ever seen.'

'. . .and the most boring,' thought Miss Savage.

'However, gardening is also about imagination and conservation. The delicately balanced life cycle of nature cannot compete with pesticides and bulldozers. What struck us most about this haven of deep cool greenery was the clever use of plants and shrubs, growing as nature intended, in perfect harmony with birds, animals and insects. Indeed it is said that Nature reserves her treasures for those who walk quietly amid. . .'

He was interrupted by a fit of raucous coughing from a raging Ivy ffrench-Fawcett, which obliterated his closing remarks.

'Therefore . . .' Mr. Savage finally arrived at the

moment everybody had been waiting for,' it has been decided unanimously that Ms. Petunia Pennefeather is the outstanding winner of the "Most Beautiful Garden" competition.'

It was difficult to decide who was the most surprised — the utterly amazed Petunia or the utterly outraged Ivy.

As she received her prize, a man with thick horn-rimmed glasses, the head of features at the XYZ TV station, drew her aside. What about a TV programme, *The World of Petunia Pennefeather,* with her as star, natch, covering plants, herbal recipes, cures for everything from blackleg to blisters, plasters to pets...?

'Oh, no,' thought Furball, covering his head.

'Do you think I could?' pouted Petunia.

'Petunia, honey,' said Billy J. Moulder, 'you're a natural ... or my name's not Billy J. Moulder!'

Miss Ivy ffrench-Fawcett stalked up the lane muttering furiously, 'That Penny Pennefeather Pondweed. Well, if she thinks I'm going to let her get away with this, she has peanut brittle for brains!'

12
Escape!

The children found the witch's new-found stardom added up to more and more work. Some days they did practically nothing but sharpen pencils for her to sign hundreds of autographs. The doorbell rang constantly. Someone had to sit by the phone all day — just in case some VIP rang. Her clothes had to be perfect at all times. And they were expected to provide meals and afternoon tea for all her television friends, at all hours of the day and late into the night. Her constant posing and pouting around the cottage became insufferable.

Furball was just as confused. He didn't know quite what to make of the witch these days. He remembered the time she had singed all his fur during a home-made gunpowder experiment. True, she had blown off her own eyebrows and half a ringlet — but that was *her* affair; she had no right to order *him* to 'test pilot' her new invention for automatic flying, and he was determined not to be used again. Yet, he had heard her muttering yesterday about trying more experiments!

He had several hard thinking sessions. A cat — even a witch's cat — had its limits.

Late one night, in front of the fading fire, the children huddled and grumbled.

'My fingers ache,' moaned Tansy, 'I must have made hundreds of cucumber sandwiches. And no thanks! All she ever says is, "Wafer thin, if you please. Take back those disgusting doorsteps." '

'It's in and out of the shops all day,' complained Joey. 'Because she won't order enough at a time.'

'I'm sick of washing and ironing her two dresses — just because she's too mean to buy any new ones,' raged Vicky. 'Well, I've had enough! I'm not going to put up with being ordered about like a common servant. Next chance I get, I'm off . . . there must be somewhere better than here.'

'Please let us come,' begged the others eagerly, and Furball miaowed appealingly as if to say, 'Me, too, please!'

As the days passed, the idea of escape grew more and more appealing. So one fine misty morning, Furball carefully closed his book for the last time. Taking a last look around the cottage, he scrambled down the wooden stairs to the waiting children.

'Hurry, Furball,' whispered Tansy impatiently. 'We've got to go before the witch wakes up with a nasty hangover again.'

Hurry, Furball.

They crept very quietly out of the door and down the path to the lane. Furball held his tail very high; he was escaping from the famous Petunia Pennefeather

at last, and was going to see the world, just like his
dear old Da.

As they shut the gate behind them, a well-known
voice cackled, 'And just where do you think you lot
are going? Hey, Tattyfur ... going to join the navy?
Tee, hee,' sniggered Petunia.

The children jumped in fright, wondering how she
always managed to know exactly what they were doing.

'We're going away,' said Vicky bravely, 'to a better
place, I'm sure.'

The witch's face grew pale! Her eyes grew beadier!
Her grey ringlets greyer!

'Listen, you lot! You can't go now. I need you here
for my most important career move.'

Furball and the children continued to walk up the
lane. They were not going to stay — and that was that.

'It's the chance of a lifetime,' yelled PP after them.

But they kept right on walking — they weren't going
to listen to anything.

'But,' yelled the witch. 'But ... we're going to be
in a movie.'

'Hrrmp,' thought the cat. 'She surely must have bats
for brains if she thinks anyone would put *her* in a
movie.'

'A last remake of *The Last Days of Petunia*,' sneered
Vicky before she could stop herself.

Petunia raced up the lane, landing in front of the
children with a thud. They stopped in surprise.

'It's a movie with Superman ...' she wheedled.

Furball stared closely at the witch and the witch
stared ever so closely at Furball (actually she squinted,
on account of her terribly poor sight).

The children looked as if they were torn in a silent
battle amongst themselves. Curiosity about the

Superman movie and loss of patience with the witch's insufferable behaviour struggled in their young faces. Finally Tansy could keep still no longer. Bouncing up and down, she cried out, 'Are you really going to make a movie with Superman, Petunia?'

Drawing herself up to her full height (which even then only measured 4ft 11ins or 1.498m) the witch scoffed nonchalantly, 'Of course! Is it so surprising, pests?'

Twanging one of her ringlets, she went on, 'I knew it would only be a matter of time before some of my natural talents were discovered. . .'

'Discovered?' thought the little grey cat. 'More like dug up from days-of-yore.'

Seeing that she had the children's undivided attention, she whipping a folding deckchair out of the hedge (left behind from the great pothole clean-up) and sat down, dabbing her eyes pitifully.

'Jeepers,' thought Furball, 'she's better at acting than I thought.'

Lifting a tearful eye from the corner of a large grey handkerchief she began again in a woeful voice.

'It's the chance of a lifetime, you see,' she sniffed loudly, causing the children to feel concern. 'You must know I simply adore Superman — the last of the REAL Hollywood stars. A star above all others,' she crooned.

'That's just because the old pair of red pyjamas can fly,' yawned Furball to himself.

Petunia went on to explain, between tears, how she had overheard Mr. Billy J. Moulder on the phone to Nutgrove Studio — in connection with interviewing up and coming starlets for the part of Superman's Granny.

'A small part in the movie?' queried Vicky.

'Well, biggish-small,' corrected PP hastily. 'The

Granny has to rescue Superman who's trapped on a diving-board twenty metres high. It's a part made to measure.' The only small requirement, it seemed, was that the actress had to *fly*.

'Fly?' gasped the children. 'As in "Move off the ground."'

Petunia sobbed painfully into a sodden handkerchief (she had learned how to do this while backstage one night, waiting for Billy J. Moulder to arrive with her pay cheque). Great big tears tumbled down her pale face as she croaked, 'And of course I would get the part with flying colours . . . if only I could fly. . .'

What a sight she was, all dull and damp and tearful. The children were quite upset at seeing the mean bad-tempered old witch appear almost human. They gathered in a huddle and whispered among themselves, interrupted every so often by loud howls of crying from Petunia.

'Hurry up. Let's decide,' urged Tansy. 'Shall we stay and make the best of it for now?'

'I'm not sure I can stand any more of this serving

and bowing and scraping ... I mean, it's not as if I had been born to it ...' Vicky looked down at the others, her normally bright face suddenly gloomy.

'Maybe she'll get us parts in the film,' suggested Joey, his face aglow.

Everyone looked at Vicky. A reluctant grin appeared. 'Well, it *is* exciting! I mean, it's not like living in an ordinary house, is it?'

The witch startled them by jumping up suddenly and shouting, 'What's the time? What's the time? I'll be late for the audition,' and she raced up the lane towards the cottage.

'But you still can't fly,' hollered the children, racing after her.

Poor Furball heaved a deep sigh and trotted after then, his dreams as downcast as his tail.

13

A Star is Born

At two minutes to two, the door of PP's bedroom creaked open. Petunia appeared, swamped in heavy stage make-up and grease-paint. She had on a pair of grey track-suit leggings under a long black cloak, and she was carrying a crash helmet.

Furball thought he would surely explode with laughter.

'Right!' she barked, forgetting her bereft-witch-in-tears act. 'Out of my way, pests. A star is about to be born!'

Watching her race out through the door the children wondered if Superman would survive the movie with Petunia. She would make Lex Luther look like Grizzly Adams.

'Let's follow her,' said Tansy, 'and see how she does at the audition.'

'I can't wait for another good laugh,' chuckled Vicky, 'Such ham acting.'

Meanwhile Petunia arrived at Nutgrove Studio, only to have the door opened by Ivy ffrench-Fawcett.

'Come to audition for tea-lady?' sniped Fiddleleaf.

'No,' snapped PP. 'To ask you to appear on my diet programme as The Wishful Shrinker.'

They growled at each other — until they caught sight of a row of young, lovely, lissome actresses, all sitting in a row. They, too, were waiting to audition.

'Snooks and tail-spins,' grumbled Petunia. 'Disgraceful! They're all the wrong age for Superman's

Granny . . . but is that going to stop them being chosen. No! Artistic integrity, my left foot.'

'How are we going to get a look in with that lot?' wailed Ivy, coming straight to the point. 'Look at that blonde hair.'

'And those rows and rows of pearly teeth. . .' put in PP disgustedly.

'They're all so slim and agile,' sobbed Ivy.

Petunia snapped her fingers. 'Time,' said she, 'time for a touch of witch-like conspiracy!'

They opened the nearest door (which was a cleaning and supply room) and tumbled inside, intent on thinking up some dastardly plan.

Much mutterings and many moochings later, they reappeared, dressed as cleaning ladies, pushing mop buckets. As they neared the waiting row of pretty actresses, Petunia began, 'Morning, ladies,' in a most friendly manner. 'Did Otis B. Henneberry explain that he wants you to audition wearing overalls and carrying mop buckets?'

The actresses seemed extremely puzzled and asked all at once, 'Overalls? Mopheads? In a Superman movie?'

'Well, not many people know this, but Superman's Granny was a simple charwoman,' went on Ivy quickly.

'And,' continued the helpful Petunia, 'and, of course, you know how eccentric these Hollywood film-makers are. For Otis B., everything has to be authentic . . . you know . . . real overalls, real mopheads. Ah, that must be himself I hear arriving. . .'

On hearing the Otis B. Henneberry Rolls pull up outside, the actresses jumped up in a panic asking, 'Where is Wardrobe . . . where can we be fitted?'

Petunia and Ivy smiled toothily, and then went on

in very confidential tones, 'Just follow us, dearies! We'll take you. . .'

The actresses filed into the cleaning-supplies room and, as soon as they were in, Petunia and Ivy flung themselves at the door and locked them in.

They raced up the corridor, dropping overalls here and mopheads there, beaming roundly.

'Shame it's such a stout door,' giggled Ivy.

'Think of the fun they'll have shining each other's teeth and jewellery at the same time,' sniggered Petunia.

They were sitting side by side in the studio as Mr. Otis B. Henneberry came in. Two assistants, carrying files, followed.

'Good morning, ladies, we shall begin auditions now. Who's first?'

One of the assistants stepped forward. 'Miss Dotty Parkon?' he chimed.

'Er . . . modelling swimwear in Malaysia,' quipped PP.

'Miss Meribel Creep?'

'Ahem . . . married in Mexico,' chipped in Ivy quickly.

'Ms. Elsbeth Tatler? Miss Boobra Friesland?'

'Mistaken for mail robbers and in jail in Manila,' shouted the witches together.

'And Malison Moody, leading lady of that great movie, *Live and Let Fly?*'

'Misplaced for meddling in microfilm,' responded PP, before falling off the seat in convulsions of laughter.

Otis B. was almost dumbstruck. Never in all his years as the great and all-powerful director of Hollywood's big-budget movies had such a thing happened to him. He was holding an audition devoid of the statutory star-struck starlets.

He shouted for his team of assistants but they had cunningly disappeared into thin air.

Otis B. rubbed his wiry beard, adjusted his silk cravat and squinted at PP and Ivy. It looked as if his boast that he could make anyone act was about to be tested.

'Odd,' he mused to himself, beckoning the two survivors to follow him to the mock-up set. 'Extremely odd, that! Spooky, almost . . .'

'Now, ladies,' began the floor manager. 'I want you both to take off from opposite sides of the studio and land on the diving-board up there. Just as if you were going to save Superman. Right! All clear? Right! Now shake hands . . . and may the best witch win!'

Ivy smirked confidently as she took PP's hand. 'Old Petunia couldn't fly to save her elbow,' she thought to herself knowingly. 'It's in the bag! The name in lights! The modelling assignments! The millions of dollars! Tee, hee. . .'

Petunia, turning her back, hurriedly pushed a parcel, with 'Fly-it-Yourself' written on the outside, up her cloak. It had been guaranteed to work or money back within 90 days. Plus free medical costs.

'Now!' shouted Otis B. 'Now, I want you to take off on the count of three! One . . . Two . . . Three . . . ACTION!'

Pulling a cord under her cloak which inflated a vest rather like a giant life-jacket, Petunia suddenly soared up and up and up. . .

'Miss ffrench-Fawcett,' screamed Otis B. 'You've missed your cue. NOW!'

Ivy, who had delayed take-off so as to have the pleasure of seeing PP crash to the ground, watched open-mouthed as she shot past, causing the priceless tooth to shiver and shake in the down-draught.

'Miss ffrench-Fawcett,' screamed Otis B. in a still louder voice, 'You're missing your cue. NOW!'

Completely disoriented and fussed, Ivy flung herself on her broomstick without remembering any of the correct take-off procedures, causing herself to zoom round and round until she was quite dizzy. Then she crashed heavily upon a poor unsuspecting cameraman, who was equally dizzy from trying to follow her progress.

'Cut!' yelled Otis B. excitedly, 'Congratulations, Miss Pennefeather. Such ... such panache ... such creative stuntwork. You have the part in the next Superman movie!' Stepping over Ivy's prostrate form, he snapped, 'Send for an ambulance, somebody ... beats me how some of these dames get equity cards.'

Petunia hugged herself, gasping delightedly, 'I did it! I did it! I flew! And at last I found a do-it-yourself kit that did it!'

Otis B. and the assistants who, seeing that all was well, had come out of the woodwork, fussed and flattered Petunia until she felt chuffed with herself and

her great notions of being a movie star. She put her
magical problems right to the back of her mind, as she
sipped champagne and spoke in most knowledgeable
terms of work permits and tax shelters.

The children, who had observed the entire carry-on
from behind the great camera tripods, were really
stunned. It appeared that the weird and wonderful
Petunia Pennefeather could confound the norms of
reasonable behaviour.

'Life with Petunia ... it's a bit like taking part in
Tales of the Unexpected,' thought Vicki.

As they trundled home together, they talked of
Hollywood and London, of greasepaint and reviews in
the paper, of their favourite stars...

They had forgotten all about Ivy ffrench-Fawcett,
who had been taken away to hospital raging at the
ambulance attendant. 'I'll fix Petunia! I'll fix her for
once and for all,' she yelled before the injection knocked
her out. 'I'll cook her goose ... I'll tell her fans ...
zzzz ...'

'Perhaps we might get to act in the movie, PP?' wheedled Vicky, as Petunia practised her landing procedures from every ditch and hedgerow on the way.

'Oh, do you think we could?' chorused Tansy and Joey, as they picked her up again after another sloppy landing in another mud bank.

'Hah,' chortled the witch. 'I may be able to get one of you a small part ... extras perhaps ... I have the producer eating out of my hand after my expert flight ... my first-class knowledge of technical equipment ... my long experience of ...'

Her eye suddenly fell on the downcast Furball. The little cat stood pawing designs in the mud, sad and silent, waiting for the usual attack of stinging remarks from old PP. But she was looking at him warmly (well, sort of lukewarm, really). 'Perhaps Furball too,' she said softly. 'After all, a witch without a cat would look pretty silly. Must ask my PRO man if it might help my image...' She droned on and on, insufferable as ever, as Furball shuddered.

Outside the big old gate of Dockleaf Cottage, everyone stopped and hesitated. Joey, deciding that he too had a flair for the dramatic, threw himself against it spouting, 'To be entering! Or not to be? That is the question.' Vicky looked at Tansy with a deep grimace before pushing it open. Tansy, following her, sighed before a grin escaped unchecked at the thought of further episodes of the Unexpected.

'Perhaps,' Furball thought, as he too turned into Dockleaf Cottage, clutching his *Great Escapes* tightly. 'Perhaps ... perhaps ... After all, tomorrow is another day ...'

TERRY MYLER trained at the National College of Art in Dublin, and also studied under her father, Sean O'Sullivan, RHA. She specialises in illustration and has done a lot of work for The Children's Press. Titles include *The Silent Sea, Save the Unicorns, Fionuala the Glendalough Goat, Murtagh and the Vikings, The Derrynalushca Dragon, the Secret of the Ruby Ring, The Witch who couldn't* and *The Witch at Batsford Castle*, the *Cornelius Rabbit* series, and Tom McCaughren's *'Legend'* books.

She lives in the Wicklow hills with her husband, two dogs and a cat. She has one daughter.

TERRY HASSETT HENRY, LTCL, NCEA, has been teaching for ten years, covering all aspects of speech and drama, and is also involved in writing and producing material for school plays, pantomines, learning techniques. She works with children of all ages, and is currently concentrating on Montessori teaching for young children.

She is married to Christopher and has two daughters, Victoria and Chloe. Greatest ambition — to rid the world of dull gloomy books for children.